BLOCK AND
ROCK

BY JAKE MADDOX

text by
Blake Hoena

STONE ARCH BOOKS
a capstone imprint

Jake Maddox JV books are published by Stone Arch Books
A Capstone Imprint
1710 Roe Crest Drive
North Mankato, Minnesota 56003
www.mycapstone.com

Library of Congress Cataloging-in-Publication Data is available on the Library of
Congress website.

ISBN: 978-1-4965-4942-6 (library binding)
ISBN: 978-1-4965-4944-0 (paperback)
ISBN: 978-1-4965-4946-4 (eBook PDF)

Summary:
Back before junior high, Justin, Tony, and Miles were the best of friends. Then they got
pigeonholed into cliques and Justin was thrown in with the band nerds while Tony and
Miles became a part of the jocks. But now that Justin wants to try out for the football
team, music and football and stereotypes begin to collide.

Editor: Nate LeBoutillier
Art Director: Russell Greismer
Designer: Kayla Rossow
Media Researcher: Eric Gohl
Production Specialist: Tori Abraham

Photo Credits:
Shutterstock: Air Images, back cover, 4, 20, 32, 42, 64, 84, David Lee, chapter openers
(background), Billion Photos, cover

Printed and bound in Canada.
010392F17

TABLE OF CONTENTS

CHAPTER 1

JAMMING

"Count us in," Miles said, turning to Justin.

Justin sat behind his drum set — just a bass, a snare, a tom-tom, and a crash cymbal. Tony and Miles stood on either side of him.

Justin raised his drumsticks high above his head and shouted, "We are The End Zonez!" Then, rapping his sticks together, he counted off, "One! Two! Three! Four!"

Justin pounded a steady beat.

Tony began to strum bar chords thick with heavy distortion.

Miles joined in with a thundering bass riff before stepping up to the mic to sing.

Oh, she was thirteen,

And a drama queen,

Hail Mary!

I was a cornerback

Defending the pass

Hail Mary!

The trio jammed in Miles' parents' garage under the flicker of fluorescent lights. Rusty tools rattled as the trio banged out song after song. The stench of motor oil and sweat hung in the air. Even though it was a sunny summer day, the garage door was closed to muffle the sound so that the neighbors would not complain.

After a few tunes, The End Zonez took a break. Miles set down his bass and went to open the garage door. Tony grabbed a football from a bin in the corner.

"Catch," he said, tossing the ball to Justin.

Justin fumbled his drumsticks, and they rattled on the concrete floor as he caught the ball. Then he lobbed it to Miles, who was pulling a Gatorade from a cooler.

"Anyone else want one?" Miles asked, holding up a bottle.

Between chugs of Gatorade, they tossed the ball around in the back alley.

At one point, Miles shouted to Justin, "Go deep."

Justin was the tallest of the trio. He turned and took off with loping strides. Tony ran after him. Gravel crunched underfoot as they sped down the alley.

Justin had a head start, but Tony was faster. He darted in front of Justin as Miles launched the ball in a high-arching pass.

Tony backpedaled to get under the ball. Just before it dropped into his hands, Justin turned and leaped, reaching up with one hand. The ball hit his palm and stuck with a loud *smuck!*

As he stumbled backward and fell, Justin tucked the ball into his chest.

"Aw, man," Tony groaned. "Thought I had the interception."

Miles jogged over, offered Justin a hand, and pulled him up off the ground.

"That was a pretty good OBJ impersonation," he said.

"OBJ?" Justin asked.

"Yeah, Odell Beckham Jr.," Tony chuckled.

"He plays for the Giants, right?" Justin said.

Tony nodded and patted Justin on the back.

"That catch reminded me of when we played peewee together," Miles said, bumping fists with Justin.

"You were always tough to defend," Tony said.

Then Tony took off down the alley. "Hit me," he shouted, raising one hand.

Justin patted the ball and chucked a wobbly pass as far as he could.

Tossing the ball around, the friends forgot about their instruments in the garage.

Justin considered summer days spent hanging out with Tony and Miles the best. They reminded him of old times, back before junior high. The three of them had lived in the same neighborhood and had known each ever since they could remember. Once upon a time, they did practically everything together.

When Tony and Miles joined peewee league football, Justin got his mom to sign him up too. They played every summer, sometimes on the same team and sometimes against each other.

When Justin's mom bought him his first drum kit, Tony and Miles begged their parents to get them instruments too. Soon they had a power trio called The End Zonez. They jammed every chance they got. Justin knew the good times were about to end. Summer was waning. School started in a couple of weeks.

While growing up, the three boys had football and music in common. But Miles and Tony were always a little more into sports than Justin, and that caused them to drift apart in junior high. With the extra demands of junior high homework, Justin had given up football to join band. Justin had always been a little more into music than his friends were.

At school, the athletes did not hang out with the band kids and vice versa. Tony and Miles might grunt a hello or nod in his direction when they passed in the hallways. But they didn't sit next to Justin in class or hang out during lunch. They spent their time with the other athletes.

CHAPTER 2

A CRAZY IDEA

"I got it," Tony said, jumping up to catch a pass from Justin. He threw the ball underhanded to Miles.

"Come, on," Miles said, motioning toward the garage. "We should pack up our gear."

With the sun setting, Miles tucked the ball under his arm. They headed back inside.

"Ready for next Wednesday?" Miles asked Tony.

"Yeah, can't wait," Tony replied.

"What's Wednesday?" Justin asked.

Tony rolled his eyes, but Miles replied, "The start of football tryouts."

As he broke down his drum set, Justin listened to his friends chat. Their school's football team was good. Last fall they had made it to playoffs but lost in the quarterfinals.

"This year, we're going all the way," Tony said.

"Yeah, conference champs!" Miles added, high-fiving Tony.

Listening to his friends, Justin felt left out. It wouldn't be until next summer, maybe, that he would have this time, this closeness with them again. After the football season, there was basketball and then baseball. And Justin would have band year-round.

"Maybe I should try out for football this year," Justin blurted.

His friends stopped in mid-conversation.

"Seriously?" Tony said.

"What about band?" Miles asked.

"I dunno," Justin shrugged. "I could still do band when the season's over."

Tony turned to Miles and snickered. "Can you see Band Boy here running down the field?" He started marching around the garage and pretending to beat a bass drum. "Ba-dum, ba-dum, ba-dum!"

Miles looked uncomfortably from Tony to Justin before starting to wrap up the cord to his amp. "Come on, hurry up," he said. "My dad will want to park the car in the garage soon."

"Mind if I come back for the rest of my gear tomorrow?" Justin asked. He was holding the case for his tom-tom in one hand with his snare in the other and a couple stands tucked under his arms. But that wasn't even half of his gear. Thankfully, he lived only a couple blocks away.

"Yeah, yeah," Miles said. "Just move everything out of the way for my dad."

Before Justin could do anything, Tony kicked Justin's cymbal. It skidded across the cement floor and rattled loudly when it hit the far wall.

"Hey, what was that for?" Justin asked.

"Just trying to help," Tony said, never looking over at Justin.

"Just go," Miles said to Justin. He picked up the bass drum and set it down next to the cymbal. "I'll take care of it."

Justin didn't know what to say about the sudden tension. He stared at his friends for a moment. "Okay," he finally said. "Guess I'll get the rest of my gear tomorrow."

"Yeah, yeah, see ya," Miles said.

As Justin walked off, he heard Tony and Miles speaking in hushed tones.

It was a difficult walk home. Not only were his arms loaded with gear, but his feeling were hurt. His friends had totally dismissed his idea of trying out for the football team. Maybe it *was* a crazy idea, and he should just stick to band. That's what people expected of him.

But what about the grab I made? he thought.

Thinking back to that catch, he couldn't help but smile. It had been a long time since he and his friends played football together. Not just catch in the alley, but played on an organized team. They had so much fun back in peewee League. Justin always liked the excitement of making a big play, and that catch reminded of his time playing wide receiver. It also gave him confidence that he still had it.

Plus if their team was as good as Miles and Tony thought, Justin might get a piece of football glory. He might get to play in the state tournament.

The next morning, Justin woke when his phone beeped. He grabbed it off his nightstand and read the text.

We haven't played all summer, so how about today? It was Char, a friend from school. She played saxophone, and they were in band together.

Shortly after that, he heard another beep, followed by the text, *Watchya doing tonight?*

It was from Brandon, a keyboard player he knew.

Justin sat up in bed and yawned before replying. He figured the two were teaming up on him. At the end of last school year, Char, Brandon, and Justin had talked about playing together more often during the summer. They didn't want to get rusty. But, for one reason or another, their plans always fell through. Probably because Justin usually ended up jamming with Miles and Tony instead.

Let me check with my mom, he texted to Char.

Char and Brandon lived on the other side of town. He would need to pick up the rest of his gear from Miles' garage and get a ride to get Char's.

After his mom agreed to drive him, he texted, *Sure, I can make it after dinner,* to Char. Then he texted, *Jamming with you and Char*, to Brandon.

Great! See you at Char's, came Brandon's instant reply.

While Miles and Tony were his best friends outside of school, Char and Brandon were his best friends at school. They sat together at lunch, often had the same classes, and were all hoping to be in jazz band together in the coming school year.

Secretly, Justin wanted feedback on what they thought about his trying out for football. During a jam break later on, Justin brought it up.

"Seriously?" Char asked, squinting at him. They were playing in her parents' basement.

"Why would you give up on the music?" Brandon asked. He sat behind his synthesizer.

"I wouldn't be giving up," Justin tried to explain. "I'd rejoin once football season ends."

"I just can't picture you walking around and grunting with those Neanderthals," Brandon said. He stood up and hunched his shoulders. He started lumbering around the basement like some uncoordinated caveman and grunted, "Throw me ball! Throw me ball!"

"Stop it!" Char said while turning away from Justin and trying to hide a grin.

Justin sat there with drumsticks in hand, not sure what to say or think. Everyone thought that since he played band last year, in seventh grade, he had to stick with it. Any change in plans was, well, crazy. Justin couldn't quite buy into the idea.

That night, on the ride home, Justin told his mom about his idea.

"I'm thinking of trying out for football this year," he said.

"That's great," she said. "Are there any permission forms I need to fill out?"

"Um, yeah. I think they're all on the school website," he said. That really was not the response he expected from his mom, not after how his friends had acted earlier.

His mom must have sensed his confusion. She added, "It's nobody's choice but your own if you play football or be in band. I'll support you."

Justin looked down at his feet. "Thanks, Mom," he said.

Right then, Justin made a pact with himself. Maybe his friends did not understand why he wanted to tryout for football. He was not really sure he understood it either. But he wanted to give it a try. If he didn't make the team, no big deal. He wouldn't have any regrets.

If he made the team, he would have a decision to make.

CHAPTER 3

TRYOUTS

With his mom's help, Justin got all the needed permission forms filled out. He went to the doctor to get a physical, and everything checked out fine. Everything was set. There was nothing to stop him except his own doubt.

Leading up to tryouts, Justin did not hear much from Miles or Tony. He sent a group text saying, *Hey, tryouts start Wednesday, right?*

Miles responded, *Yeah.*

What time? he asked.

Ten, Tony replied.

That was it. No *See ya there!* No show of
support from his old friends. It kind of felt like
they were already back at school, and his friends
were ignoring him.

That did not help his confidence. He had
not played football since peewee, and he knew
he would be rusty. Sure, he had played catch
with Tony now and then. But playing catch and
catching a pass during a game were two completely
different things.

Char and Brandon also seemed to be avoiding
him. They knew that if he made the team, football
practice would take the place of band practice. But
still, he was hoping for a little support. Justin was
beginning to feel that all of his friends were quietly
waiting for him to fail.

The morning of the first practice, Justin woke
early. His parents worked early, so he was on his
own. After breakfast, he hopped on his bike and
headed out with a duffle bag slung over his back.

After pedaling a couple of miles to the school, Justin locked up his bike in the rack and walked over to the football field. There were already a few dozen other kids gathered on the bleachers. Returning eighth-graders sat up top while the new seventh-graders sat at the bottom.

Justin was not sure where to sit. He didn't really know any of the seventh-graders. Yet, looking up at the eighth-graders, he thought most of them felt like strangers too. They were the athletes. They were not kids he had ever hung out with at school. Justin did see Miles and Tony sitting up toward the top of the bleachers, but they were surrounded by other eighth-graders.

Feeling completely out of place, Justin found a seat about halfway up and off to the side. As he sat down, he heard a few mumbles coming from the eighth-graders. Justin tried to ignore them. Later, the team's head coach, Mr. Matthews, stepped across the field. Some assistant coaches followed.

"For those of you who played JV last year," Mr. Matthews called out to the eight-graders, "shout out your name and the position you played."

As they did the rounds, Miles yelled, "Miles Evans, linebacker."

Tony shouted, "Tony McDaniels, cornerback."

"The rest of you," the coach said, turning to the remaining kids, "shout out your name and the position you'd like to play. If you make the team, I can't promise you'll get that position. But it'll give us an idea where to start you off."

When it was Justin's turn, he called out, "Justin Thomas, wide receiver."

Justin heard some snickers again. He turned to see Tony joking with some of the other defensive backs. A couple of them were looking his way.

Once Coach had gotten all their names, half of the kids went to one side of the field to work on playing defense. The other half took the opposite end of the field to practice offense.

As Justin was walking away, someone slammed a shoulder into him, spinning him around. Justin turned to see Tony and a couple of the defensive backs. He wasn't exactly sure which of them had bumped him.

Justin stood there for a moment, not sure what to say or do. Tony, laughing and smiling, walked off without turning around. For a second, Justin thought of turning, walking the other direction, getting on his bike, and heading home.

Then Justin heard his name. Coach Johnson, an older, grizzled assistant who worked with the offense, was shouting at him. Justin ran over.

"Okay, Thomas," Coach Johnson said. "We're going to time your forty-yard dash."

Justin lined up with the other wide receiver hopefuls. One by one, they waited for Coach Johnson to say, *Ready, set, go!* Then they took off, sprinting down the field as another coach with a stopwatch recorded the time.

Most of the other kids were posting times between five and five-and-a-half seconds. Justin's time was one of the slowest at 5.63 seconds.

They proceeded to running tires and cones. Every drill was timed, and there was always an assistant jotting notes on a clipboard. Justin kept feeling like he was a step or two behind the other guys.

After the first part of practice, they were given a break to get some water. Justin tried using the break to talk to Miles and Tony. But they were hanging out with some of the other defensive players. He couldn't get close to them.

The second part of practice went much smoother for Justin. The offensive players were further divided into positions: quarterbacks, linemen, running backs, and wide receivers.

Justin went with the receivers and worked on passing drills. That is where he shined. He had strong arms and hands from banging on drums.

Justin snagged almost every ball thrown his way. Other kids were bobbling the ball and dropping passes.

Afterward, Coach Johnson patted him on the back. He said, "You got some great mitts, Thomas."

That put a smile on Justin's face despite his earlier struggles.

As he walked to his bike, Justin looked for his friends. But the eighth-graders who were on the team last year stayed behind to meet with the coaches. He saw Miles and Tony standing with them. Justin figured it would be awkward, just standing around and waiting for them. Plus, he wasn't sure they even wanted to talk to him. Justin decided to sling his duffle bag over his shoulder and leave.

Only later did he receive a text from Miles saying, *How'd it go?*

Ok, I think, Justin texted. *I'm beat.*

Just wait ;), Miles texted back.

The next day, Justin groaned as he got out of bed. He was surprisingly sore, and he hadn't even thrown a block or taken a hard tackle. All he'd done is run around. Problem was, he hadn't run around that much in forever.

The following practice was more of the same. The team started off with warm-ups and some timed drills. He always felt like he was a step behind the other wide receiver hopefuls. After finishing last, again, during one drill, he heard some laughter as he bent over to suck in gasps of air. Tony's group of defensive backs watched him. Justin did his best to ignore them.

Friday came. As Justin walked over to join the receivers, one of the assistants yelled to him, "Thomas, you're with the linemen today."

Joining the linemen, Justin quickly realized some major differences. While most of the linemen were shorter than he was, they were bulkier and stronger. They also knew what they were doing.

After warm-ups, the linemen worked on hand and foot coordination drills with Coach Johnson. They moved on to blocking drills.

At one point, Justin was down in a three-point stance for drive drills. Another kid, Andre, stood in front of him holding a large blocking pad. The assistant shouted, "Ready, set, hut!"

Justin jumped up from the stance, smacked the pad with his hands, and tried to shove Andre backward. Andre hardly budged.

"Thomas, don't push with your arms," Coach Johnson yelled. "Once you hit the pad, get your feet moving. Drive him back with your legs!"

Justin tried it again, using the coach's advice. It worked a little better, using his lower body. The problem was that Andre was like a large boulder.

The linemen went on to mirror drills. On the snap of the ball, the offensive linemen were supposed to try to mirror the defensive linemen's moves. The had to stay balanced and not back down.

Justin was put on offense and got down in his stance. Andre stood in front of him. Coach Johnson yelled, "Ready, set, hut!" Andre started to move from side to side, as if he were trying to rush the quarterback. Justin broke out of his stance and held up his hands to copy Andre's movements and block him from advancing.

Justin shuffled from side to side, trying to stay in front Andre, who was surprisingly quick for his size. When Andre juked one way and went the other, Justin got caught flat-footed. He tripped over his own feet and ended up on his backside.

Andre smiled.

"Keep your feet moving, Thomas, even when you're standing in one spot," growled Coach Johnson. "Get down in your stance and try again."

Justin and Andre went at it again. This time Justin lasted longer, but Andre still got by him.

Justin shook his head.

"Again," said Coach Johnson. "You'll get it."

Justin tried a couple more times with mixed success. He watched the other linemen try the drill after that, hoping to learn as quickly as possible. Most of what Justin was asked to do was new to him. He always felt like he was a step behind.

At the end of practice, all of the players sat in the bleachers so the coaches could address them together. Like before, the eighth-graders sat toward the top, the seventh-graders at the bottom.

Justin sat in the middle and off to the side. He was so worn out that it didn't bother him as much.

Coach Matthews announced, "Next week, we will be practicing in full pads, so be here a little earlier Monday morning to get suited up. It will be the last week of tryouts. The final roster will be posted the Sunday before school starts. Now, on three, Eagles. One, two, three . . ."

At the same time, everyone shouted, *Eagles!*

CHAPTER 4

WEEKEND JAM

Justin left practice without even bothering to talk to Miles or Tony. They had mostly ignored him all week. Justin didn't expect that to change, so he hopped on his bike and left.

But when he got home, he saw that he had a text from Char. *Hey, big guy. Wanna jam with Brandon and me tomorrow?*

At least Char was talking to him. He waited to make sure he could get a ride from his mom before replying, *Sure.*

That night Justin hung out at home. It was probably the first Friday night all summer that he was not over at Miles' or Tony's. He was itching to play, but he was a little beat. Also, it would be a pain to set up and tear down and re-pack his drum kit for tomorrow.

After dinner, he went up to his room. He grabbed his headphones and the drumsticks on his nightstand. He turned on Rush, some of their early stuff. They were one of the best rock trios ever, Justin thought. He liked to mimic their drummer, Neil Peart, and his aggressive style with his playing in The End Zonez. With only three members in the band, each person's role was a little more important, and a dynamic drummer was needed to carry the band.

Justin sat on his bed and air-drummed along. After a few songs, he switched to some even older Cream, with Ginger Baker as their drummer. Baker melded jazz rhythms into some classic rock tunes.

Justin was lost in his world when his door creaked open. Miles poked his head in and shouted, "Hey!"

Embarrassed, Justin dropped his sticks and pulled off his headphones.

"Hey!" he said, louder than he meant to.

Miles was all smiles when he asked, "Who you listening to?"

"Cream," Justin replied.

"That's pretty old school," Miles said as he sat down on the bed next to Justin. "Got any Black Keys or Arctic Monkeys?"

"Just check out Jack Bruce's bass riffs," Justin said, handing Miles his headphones.

Justin watched as his friend listened to the next song. Miles played air bass and mumbled along to "White Room," one of the band's hits. When the song was half-finished, Miles took off the headphones.

"How you holding up, man?" Miles said.

"I'm a little sore," Justin said. "We haven't even put on pads yet."

"Yeah, next week it gets real," Miles said.

There was a long pause. Neither friend really knew what to say, which was odd. They had hung out all summer, but school and football were uncomfortable territory for the old friends.

"I could set up my drums if you wanna play," Justin said.

"Can't tonight," Miles said, shaking his head. "Studying our defensive playbook. I'm hoping to make defensive team captain this year."

Justin bowed his head as Miles stood up and walked over to the door.

"I just wanted to check to see how you're doing," Miles said. "I saw you've been practicing with the linemen."

"Yeah, I'm not sure about that," Justin said.

"Hey, we're a running team," Miles said. "The O-line is an important piece of our offense."

Justin smiled at that. He knew what his friend was trying to do: boost his confidence. Because of things like that, Justin would be surprised if Miles did not become one of the team's captains.

"See you Monday?" Miles asked.

"Yeah, sure," Justin said.

Miles left.

Justin set his drumsticks back on his nightstand. He put on his headphones, turned his music to shuffle, and lay back in bed. Soon he drifted off to sleep.

***

Early Saturday afternoon, Justin found himself again in Char's parents' basement. He was sitting behind his three-piece drum set and banging away.

"Come on. Slow down," Brandon kept yelling.

They were just warming up. But Justin couldn't help himself. He was upset at how poorly football tryouts were going and taking it out on the drums.

Justin held his drumsticks with an overhand grip so he could pound fast and heavy on the snare drum.

Finally, Brandon mashed his hand down on his keyboard to make a loud, disrupting sound, which brought their jam session to a halt.

"We aren't a garage band," Brandon said to Justin. "Slow it down."

"I actually like the faster tempo," Char said. "But we gotta keep the volume down, or my folks won't let us practice here."

Justin set his sticks down. He buried his face in his palms. "Sorry, guys," he said, letting out a deep sigh.

Char gave Brandon a dark glance.

"What?" Brandon said. "I didn't know he'd start crying."

Justin looked up at his friend. "I'm not crying," he said. "I'm just annoyed at my friends."

"What did we do?" Char asked.

"Not you," Justin said. "Tony and Miles. They have been acting strangely. And football tryouts have been tough."

"So why are you even going out for football?" Brandon said. "I thought you knew that athletes are just jerks."

"I've known Miles and Tony since grade school," Justin said. "We go back a long way. They're not jerks."

"I thought you just said they were," said Char.

Justin sighed again. "Well, they sort of are. Well, Tony, I mean. But they didn't used to be jerks. It's just messing with me, that's all."

"If you're just going to whine about your old buddies, I'm out of here," Brandon said. He began breaking down his keyboard.

"Seriously?" Char said. "You're really leaving already, Brandon? We barely started."

"And my mom won't be back to pick me up for a couple hours," Justin added.

None of that stopped Brandon. He packed everything up in record time and left with his keyboard strapped over his shoulder. "Call me when you wise up," he said. "*If* you wise up."

"What's up with him?" Justin asked Char.

She turned to Justin and sighed. "I think he's still upset at Tony," she said.

"About what?" Justin asked.

"Don't you remember what happened last year?" she asked.

Justin shook his head. He had no idea what she was talking about.

"They got in a fight," she said. "Did you forget when Brandon showed up to practice with that shiner?"

"Yeah," Justin said. "But he told me he tripped packing up his keyboard after we were done playing."

"And you believed that?" said Char.

Justin shrugged. "Well, yeah."

"That's not what he told me," Char said. "He told me that he got it from Tony. And besides that, don't you remember all the rumors? Everyone was talking about it."

"No one told me," Justin said, turning away from her.

Justin had known Tony his whole life. While Tony could be a little harsh, especially lately, Justin had never known him to pick a fight.

CHAPTER 5

WEEK TWO

Monday morning, after getting his practice gear on and stretching out with the team, Justin was back practicing with the wide receivers. Coach Matthews ran the show. They were working on one-on-one drills with the defensive backs.

That's how Justin ended up lining up across from Tony.

"Ready, set, hut!" called out the quarterback.

Justin jumped from his stance. He was met instantly by Tony, who came in low on Justin, knocking him off balance. Justin recovered and tried running his route, but Tony was on him tight.

"Get some separation!" Coach Matthews yelled.

The quarterback tossed the ball. Justin reached out to grab it, but Tony batted it away before Justin could get his hands on it.

The same thing happened another couple times as Justin lined up against other defenders. Justin began to wonder how he would ever catch a pass if he couldn't even get open.

At one point, after knocking the ball away from Justin again, Tony barked, "Give it up, Band Boy!"

Justin paused for a moment. He looked down at the ball rolling away. Then he glared at his "friend" Tony, who wore an ugly smirk behind his facemask. A couple other defensive players stood around chuckling.

Coach Matthews wasn't impressed. "Come on. Get back to it," he snapped.

Someone picked up the ball and tossed it to the center while Justin jogged to the back of the line of wideouts.

Every time after that, whenever Justin lined up against one of the D-backs, they would make fun of him. They'd mutter something like, "Come on, Band Boy," or "Give it up, Band Boy."

It was Justin's roughest day of practice yet. Thinking back to what Char had said, he started question how well he knew Tony. If Tony could harass someone who was supposed to be his friend, he probably wouldn't have a problem picking a fight with someone like Brandon.

***

The next day at practice, Justin wasn't working out with the receivers. He was thankful for that. It meant he would not have to face Tony or any of the other defensive backs.

Justin practiced with the offensive lineman. Up until now, they had just worked on techniques. But just like with catching the ball, things changed when the situation became more game-like.

Now Justin found himself facing off against Miles. Miles mostly played linebacker, but Justin had to go after Miles when the O-line started to work on run-blocking.

Both Justin and Miles were in their stances.

The quarterback called, "Ready, set, hut!"

Justin jumped up and rushed forward. His job was to drive Miles back, to give the ball carrier room to run.

Miles met Justin's charge and then spun to the right, ducking under Justin's block. Justin got caught flat-footed as Miles ran by him.

"Keep in front of your man!" shouted Coach Matthews. "Next up."

As they walked away, Miles patted Justin on the back of the helmet. "Better luck next time," his friend said. He wasn't laughing, so Justin figured he meant it.

But things were different when he lined up against a different defender.

"Bet you can't beat me, Band Boy!" snarled a defensive end.

The QB called the signals and took the snap.

Justin rushed forward. The defender grabbed him by the shoulders pads, twisted him around, and tossed him to the ground.

Justin landed on his back. The wind was knocked from him.

"Best stay there," the defensive end mumbled as he walked off.

Justin didn't have much of a choice. He could hardly breathe. It took him a few seconds to get to his feet. Then he noticed that not only were some of the defenders snickering, but some of the offensive linemen too. He heard the name *Band Boy* spread, whispered on their breaths.

"Next up!" the assistant yelled.

In the back of his mind, Justin weighed what would be more embarrassing: continuing with the tryouts or walking off the field.

For a second, Justin thought about calling it quits. That would be the easy thing. He could just go back to playing in band, to hanging out with Char and Brandon during the school year. He could forget about playing football. Forget about getting The End Zonez back together next summer. Put the past behind him and just accept the fact that his oldest friends were no longer his best friends.

"Thomas, back of the line," said Coach Matthews.

Justin jogged back to stand with the offensive linemen. Waiting in line, Justin decided to make a deal with himself. He would finish tryouts and work his hardest to make the team. If he didn't, fine. That was up to Coach Matthews. It wasn't up to anybody else. Not Tony. Not Brandon.

The offensive line soon moved on to some live pass-blocking. This was even more difficult than run-blocking. Instead of charging forward to clear a path, the O-linemen had to keep defenders from tackling the quarterback.

After the snap, a coach would count off five seconds. *One-one thousand. Two-one thousand. Three-one thousand. Four-one thousand. Five-one thousand.* The blockers had to try to keep defenders off the quarterback so he could relax in the pocket and choose his receiver.

Justin got pushed back. He got tossed to the side. He got thrown to the ground. But he kept getting back up. He kept on trying.

After one play, Coach Johnson pulled Justin over to the quarterback, a kid named Aaron Jorgenson. He put his arms around both players and whispered, "Thomas, the next time you line up, here's what you do. After initial contact, I want you to let the defender go and run a short out route." To Jorgenson, he said, "As soon as Thomas releases the rusher, hit him with the pass."

The quarterback nodded.

As Justin got into stance, the defender across from him growled, "I'm going bury you, Band Boy."

Justin gulped.

The assistant yelled, "Ready, set, hike!"

The defender charged. Justin met his rush, but
when he juked, Justin let him get by. Then Justin
took a couple loping strides down field, turning to
the outside and looking back to the quarterback.
The ball was already on its way, and he just got his
hands up and on the ball to snag it out of the air.

Justin strutted down field a few steps before
Miles tackled him cleanly.

"Nice snag, JT," Miles shouted, helping him to
his feet and slapping him on the helmet.

As Justin ran back to the huddle, Coach
Matthews gave an approving nod. Then he
whispered something to the assistant next to him.

It was small victory for Justin, and one of the
first times he felt like he'd done anything right.

CHAPTER 6

AN ADVANTAGE

The rest of Justin's week was a blur. During some drills, Coach Matthews had him running routes with the wide receivers. Other times, Coach Johnson had him working on blocking drills with the linemen. Justin wondered where he fit in, or if he even fit on the team at all.

There also seemed to be a battle going on over his nickname. The sides were clearly drawn. When he failed at wideout, the defensive backs called him "Band Boy." If, while lined up at tight end, he snagged a pass or made a good block, the O-line called him JT.

Justin had to admit that the nickname stuff motivated him to play harder. He'd rather be called JT than Band Boy. But it wasn't that simple. He wished he knew why he struggled anytime he faced one of the defensive backs, especially Tony. Sure, it was obvious he just didn't have the pure speed to beat them. But it began to seem like a mental thing too. The D-backs were getting to him.

One time, after Tony knocked a ball out of Justin's hands, Coach Johnson called both of them over to him. Then he motioned to the quarterback to join them.

"Stand back to back," Coach Johnson said to Tony and Justin.

The friends gave each other a confused look before doing as they were told. Justin stood easily a head taller than Tony.

"Raise your arms," Coach Johnson said.

The tips of Tony's fingers barely reached above Justin's elbows.

Coach Johnson looked at Jorgenson. "Now what do you see there?" he asked.

"Um . . . that JT is taller than Tony," said the quarterback.

Coach Johnson clapped his hands together. "Bingo!" he said. "We call that a height advantage."

Jorgenson and some of the other guys laughed.

Coach Johnson frowned. "So then why are you trying to hit him in the chest with the ball?" he said. "Any little old defender can knock it away when you throw it there. Now let's line up and run that play again."

Justin went to the line of scrimmage. Tony stood across from him. Jorgenson crouched behind center and called the signals.

When Jorgenson yelled, "Hut!" Justin burst from his stance. Tony met him to knock him off his route. Justin did his best to break free and then turned back to the quarterback. Jorgenson released the ball. It sailed high.

Justin had to reach up above his head for the ball. Tony tried to bat the ball away, but it was out of his reach. Justin pulled the ball out of the air and turned to run down field. Tony had tumbled to the ground and was scrambling to get up.

Coach Johnson clapped loudly. "Way to go. Way to use your size, Thomas." Turning to Jorgenson, he added, "He's a big target with good hands. Keep throwing it where only he can catch it."

***

When Friday's practice ended, Coach had everyone gather on the bleachers again.

"Great effort, team," Coach Johnson began. "I saw some surprises out there, and the coaching staff will have some tough decisions to make. Over the weekend, I will post the roster. We will have a short team meeting after school Monday, and then practice begins on Tuesday. Now, one, two, three . . ."

Everyone shouted, *Eagles!*

Justin looked back as he started walking toward the bike racks. He saw Tony talking to some of the other defensive backs. Miles stood next to Coach Reynolds, who was in charge of special teams. They both glanced Justin's way. Miles nodded at Justin.

At that point, Justin barely cared whether he made the team or not. He was just thankful that the stress of the tryouts was over. He could have one nice, relaxing weekend before school started.

But it also turned out to be a lonely weekend for Justin. He didn't hear from Tony, not that he wanted to. Miles sent him a vague text, saying Coach Reynolds was talking about him. Justin really wasn't sure what to make of that. Char and Brandon were silent. He guessed they were probably jamming together. After the previous weekend's blowup, Justin didn't want to risk asking to join them.

Except for when his mom took him out to buy some school supplies, Justin hung out at home. He mostly stayed up in his room and listened to some of his favorite drummers, from Buddy Rich to Keith Moon.

Justin spent hours lying in bed. With his headphones on, he listened to music until it drowned out all his nagging thoughts. He drummed the air until his arms were shaky with the strain of movement.

CHAPTER 7

MAKING THE CUT

Monday morning, Justin got ready for school early. He got to the bus stop before anyone else. Since he, Miles, and Tony, lived close to each other, they rode the same bus. He hoped he could talk to his friends while they waited for their ride.

Over the weekend, Justin had been stressing about making the team. He never checked the roster online. He hated to think that making the team might affect who he hung out with and who his friends were at school.

Justin was sure that Tony and Miles would have checked. They would tell him his fate. Either they would congratulate him, or they would begin to ignore him like last year.

But Tony and Miles never showed up. Justin rode the bus to school in silence.

It was a chilly morning, so most of the kids went inside instead of standing around in the schoolyard. Justin wandered over to the cafeteria. The first person he saw was Char. She was sitting with Brandon and a couple other kids from band.

"Hey," Char said, scooting over so he could sit next to her.

"What's up?" Justin replied.

A couple of the others muttered hellos, but Brandon looked away. Justin didn't know exactly what that meant. Was Brandon still mad about the last jam session? Or maybe he heard Justin made the team. Char seemed uncomfortable with the silence. Justin didn't know what to say.

Miles and Tony walked in. They must have gotten a ride from one of their parents. As they walked through the cafeteria, some of the other defensive players joined them. They had a small entourage by the time they walked by Justin's table. Miles waved to Justin, but Tony did not even look his way. Tony glared at Brandon, who was glaring back.

"What's your problem, Band Boy?" Tony said as he walked past.

Brandon didn't respond.

Char turned to Justin. "So did you make the team?" she asked.

Before Justin could respond, Brandon blurted, "And if you did, why are you even sitting with us?"

Justin looked away under the heat of Brandon's glare. "I don't know if I made it or not," he said. "I've been afraid to look."

"Don't you think that information might be useful?" Char said.

"Why don't you just ask your Neanderthal friends over there," Brandon said, looking toward Tony and Miles.

They stood on the far side of the room now. Their group had grown larger as they smiled and laughed and joked around.

"What's your problem?" Char said to Brandon.

Brandon just got up and walked away. Justin wanted to follow, but Char grabbed his arm.

"Let him go," she said.

Soon, the bell rang, sending them to the morning's first period of classes.

Justin resisted checking the roster until halfway through algebra, second period. He got a hall pass and went to the boys' bathroom, taking his phone out of his locker on the way.

Justin logged into the school webpage and found the link for the football team roster. In addition to listing who made the cut, the coaches had set up a depth chart.

Justin scrolled down through the offensive starters but did not find his name. He scrolled down the defensive players, and saw Tony, starting cornerback, and Miles, starting inside linebacker. He also saw a C next to Miles' name, which meant he had become one of the team captains.

At the bottom was a list of players who would be playing on special teams. That meant kickoffs and punts. That's where Justin found his name. He was also listed as a backup tight end.

Justin knew enough about football to know what a tight end was, but it was a position he wasn't totally familiar with. Back in peewee league football, they never used a tight end. Justin put his phone back and went back to algebra class.

At lunch, Justin found Char and Brandon at the same table. He sat with them, though Brandon rolled his eyes and shook his head.

"So?" Char asked. "You find out yet?"

"Yeah," said Brandon. "Are you a Neanderthal?"

"I made it," he said. "I'm on special teams. I'm also a back-up tight end."

"So no band?" Char asked.

Justin shook his head and said, "No, not until after football season. But that doesn't mean we can't jam."

"When?" Brandon said.

"Games are on Fridays, so what about Saturdays?" Justin asked.

"Can't. That's when jazz band has most of it performances," Brandon said.

"Then Sundays?" Justin said. "You can't let me get too rusty."

"We'll see," Brandon said.

Just then, a tray plopped down beside Justin.

"Mind if I join you?" Miles said.

Brandon scowled. Char nodded and smiled. Justin couldn't say no to Miles.

"So what are you talking about?" Miles asked. "JT's new hobby?"

Justin smiled.

"Trying to figure out a time Justin could play with us, since he won't be in the school band," Char said.

"Need a bass player?" Miles asked.

"You can't be serious," Brandon said.

"What type of music do you play?" Char asked.

"Didn't Justin ever tell you about The End Zonez?" Miles asked. "We write a lot of our own stuff."

Justin saw Brandon roll his eyes, but Char leaned in closer as Miles talked.

CHAPTER 8

FIRST GAME

That day, after school, Justin went to the gym for the team meeting. Unlike during tryouts, the kids divided themselves into offensive and defensive players, instead of by grade.

When Justin walked by the defenders, he heard a couple snickers and "Band Boy" being whispered. But when he reached the offensive players, a few high-fived him, and said "Hey, JT."

Soon Coach Matthews walked in and launched into an overview of coming practices and games. Their first game was in two weeks. Above all, he encouraged all the players to study the playbook.

After they headed out to the practice field, Coach Johnson pulled Justin aside. "I know you wanted to be a wide receiver," he said. "You just don't have the speed to fill that role."

"Oh, I know. It's okay," Justin said, looking down at his shoes.

"But we have plans for you," the coach continued. "We intend to be a running team, which is why you aren't the starting tight end. Your blocking needs some work. But we've seen that you can catch the ball. And your height is an advantage."

Justin nodded.

Coach Johnson scratched at his grizzled whiskers. "You'll get some playing time, Thomas. Just hang in there."

"I will," said Justin.

Practice that day felt different from tryouts, just knowing he made the team. But it was still a lot of work, and Justin had a lot left to learn.

***

School was an ongoing whirlwind for Justin. It's not like Justin was the greatest student ever. He had to pay close attention to his teachers and his homework to keep afloat. Then there were choices about who to sit by in nearly every class. There was always either someone he knew from band or a member of the football team in every class he had. He felt torn.

The one person he made sure to avoid was Tony. When they saw each other in the hallway, they didn't even bother with hellos. Every now and then, they lined up against in other during practice, during a scrimmage. But Tony didn't even bother calling Justin "Band Boy" anymore. He just ran the plays and ignored his old friend.

It took some getting used to, for Justin. He tried to imagine what Tony was trying to prove, but Justin didn't come up with anything.

Then came their first game.

On game days, Coach Matthews required players to dress up in a shirt and tie. It was a tradition. Even though he had been practicing with the team for the past few weeks, many of Justin's classmates did not know he was on the football team. They were used to him being one of the drummers in band. That Friday, the shirt and tie he wore got Justin a lot of stares.

Because it was an away game, he got to leave early from his last period class. Then the team took a bus to a nearby town. In the locker room, the players exchanged their shirts and ties for shoulder pads and their white visiting uniforms.

Playing on special teams, Justin was on the field for the opening kickoff. The whistle blew, and the opposing kicker ran up to the ball and booted it. Justin watched the ball sail over his head. Behind him, the kick returner readied to catch the ball. In front of him, opposing players approached.

Kickoffs were like collisions of two charging armies. Players grunted at the contact. Pads and helmets cracked. Cleats thudded over the turf.

Justin engaged in some brief contact. Before he knew it, the whistle blew, and the play was over. It all happened so fast that Justin wasn't really sure what went on. But the refs had placed the ball at the 30-yard line, so Justin jogged off the field to let the Eagle offense take over.

That's how most of the game went for him. When his team punted, kicked, or returned, he'd line up in the tight end position, blocking any defenders from getting past him if he could. Then once he heard the distinct sound of the ball being launched sky high, he'd rush down the field to try and tackle or block some more.

It felt like a lot of running up and down the field for nothing. But every time they stopped a return or fielded a kick, Coach Reynolds was there, reminding his players of their important role.

True to Coach Johnson's word, the Eagles ran the ball a lot. From the sideline, Justin watched play after play where their quarterback would simply turn to hand the ball off. Their running back would burst through a line of bodies slamming into each other to gain a few yards.

Every now and then, they tried a short pass. But they did not equal the success of the slow and steady, grind-it-out style of running the ball.

Late in the fourth quarter of a back and forth game, Justin got a chance to play offense. The Eagles were down by four and had a fourth-and-eight situation deep in their opponent's territory.

Coach Matthews decided not to go for the field goal. Three points would not win the game. So they were going for it, and it was a passing down. That's when Coach Matthews sent Justin into the lineup.

Justin trotted up to the huddle for his first offensive play. He was even more nervous when he heard the play call.

"Eighty-four screen on three," said Jorgenson, the quarterback, in the huddle.

It was a tight end screen. That meant Justin was the intended target.

Justin lined up next to the right tackle and got down in his stance. Jorgenson called out signals. A defensive end crouched in front of Justin, wiggling his fingers, ready to rush the pass.

The center snapped the ball. The offensive linemen burst from their stances to meet them. The defensive end surged forward. Justin crashed into him, but instead of meeting him head-on, Justin put a glancing shoulder into the defensive end's chest. Then he slipped by and turned upfield to run his route, a quick out pattern.

Jorgenson released the ball. Justin saw it sail just over the defender's outstretched hand and spiral toward him. Justin reached up, watching the ball into his hands. It stuck with a satisfying *smuck*. Turning quickly, he began to run.

Justin needed another four or five yards for the first down. Suddenly, Justin felt the impact of shoulder pads crunching into his side. The contact was jarring and painful. Justin lost his grip on the ball and landed on his back. A pile of bodies landed next to him as players dove for the football.

When all was sorted out, the other team had recovered the fumble. Justin and the other offensive players jogged off field as the Eagle defense ran on. While he was heading off, he felt the smack of shoulder pads bumping into his. It was Tony.

"Way to go, Band Boy," Tony said as he ran by.

Justin felt terrible. His first pass reception and he had fumbled the ball.

Once on the sideline, Coach Johnson called him over. "Next time, tuck the ball under your arm before you start heading up the field, Thomas," he said.

Justin nodded.

At that point, there wasn't much left of the game. The other team drove it down field and ran the clock out. The Eagles lost, 28 to 24.

It was a disappointing way to start the season. In the locker room, hardly anyone said a thing. They changed quickly and headed back to the bus.

As Justin was heading out, he was met by Tony and a couple of the defensive backs.

"Nice fumble, Band Boy," one of them said.

"Your screw-up lost us the game," another said.

Justin looked to his friend for support. But Tony did nothing. Said nothing. Not even when another one of the defensive players walked by and bumped Justin into the wall.

"It's the front of the bus for you," he said as they shuffled passed him.

This was something Justin had only heard rumors about. But anyone who botched a big play was forced to sit in front of the bus.

Thing is, Justin didn't get it.

Sure, he fumbled the ball as he got tackled. But it's not like he was going to get the first down. He was a couple yards short of the sticks, and it was fourth down. The other team was going to get the ball back.

Still, when he hopped on the bus, a couple of the defensive backs were there to make sure he didn't make it past the first few rows.

Tony was one of them. Justin took a long, hard stare at his old friend. In the old days, Tony might've been the sort of guy that he could talk to about something like this.

Tony narrowed his eyes.

Justin turned and sat.

CHAPTER 9

AN OLD FRIEND

Saturday morning, Justin woke when his phone buzzed. It was a text from Tony. Probably the first one he had received since football tryouts started. All it said was, *Wanna talk? Park?*

Justin knew what Tony meant by his short text. Between his, Tony's, and Miles' houses, there was a small park. It held just a couple park benches and some swings. Three swings to be exact. It was a place they had met in the past when one of them had something to get off his chest.

They didn't use the park as much as they had when they were younger. In fact, it had been quite a while.

Give me 15, Justin replied.

Ok, Tony texted.

Justin rolled out of bed and got dressed. He grabbed a banana off the kitchen table and slugged down a glass of OJ. Then he was out the door.

It was only a short walk to the park. He thought he'd get there early to claim the middle swing. Justin was surprised that Tony was already there. He had the middle swing. That was usually reserved for the person who wanted to do the talking. Justin had wanted to get there first because he was annoyed at Tony. Gravel crunched underfoot as Justin neared the swings.

"Hey," Tony said.

"Hey," Justin replied.

Justin took a seat. They sat quietly for a moment, just swaying back and forth.

Finally, Tony said, "I'm sorry."

Justin looked at Tony. He was surprised that Tony had started with an apology. But, in another way, he was not surprised. They had been friends for years.

"It's just . . ." Tony started. "Football was supposed to be my thing. Mine and Miles' thing. You had band."

"But I thought football was our thing," Justin said. "We've always played catch together, and we had peewee league."

"No," Tony said. "You don't get it."

Justin frowned.

"Don't you remember back in peewee?" said Tony. "You were always showing me up."

"First of all, that was years ago," Justin said. "And second of all, no I didn't."

"You were always so much taller than me," Tony explained. "I could never stop you from catching the ball."

Tony put his feet down and stopped swaying for a moment. Then he pushed against the ground and swung backward. He swooped back and forth a few times.

Justin didn't know what to say.

Tony planted his feet and stopped again. Looking over at Justin, he said, "You were always a better football player *and* musician than me. I thought that once you went out for band, football could be my thing and band yours."

Jealousy? Justin thought. *Is it as simple as that? That's that what's causing Tony to act like a jerk?*

"I only tried out for football so I could hang out with you guys," Justin said. "I thought The End Zonez was our thing, but you guys never wanted to play during the school year."

"That's not true," Tony said. "I convinced Miles that we should focus on sports during the school year. We knew we could jam during the summer."

"Really? Why?" Justin asked.

"I don't know," he said. "I guess so Miles and I could hang out more."

Now it was Justin's turn to kick back on the swing and rock back and forth. After a while, he asked, "So what about Brandon?"

"What about him?" Tony asked.

"I heard you got in some kind of a fight with him," Justin said.

"From who?" Tony asked. "I remember him bumping into me after one of our games. He tripped and fell over some of his gear. Think he smacked himself while trying to pick everything up. Kind of funny actually."

"So you never hit him?" Justin asked.

"Come on. You've known me forever," Tony said. "When have I ever gotten into a fight?"

That is when Justin had another crazy idea. One that might be just as crazy as trying out for the football team.

"What if we added a keyboardist and a sax player to The End Zonez?" Justin asked.

***

Justin felt better knowing why Tony had been acting like such a jerk lately. But that made him realize he had one other friendship to work on: his friendship with Brandon.

On Monday, Justin cornered Brandon at his locker.

"What do you want?" Brandon said.

"Wanna join The End Zonez?" Justin asked.

He had already talked to Miles and Char about his latest crazy idea. They were both on board. Secretly, Justin thought it was because they were crushing on each other. Brandon was the last friend he had to talk to about it.

"Seriously, The End Zonez?" Brandon asked. "That's a stupid name."

"So, do you want in?" Justin said.

"But I don't like football," Brandon continued.

Justin sighed. Brandon was being evasive, so Justin cut to the chase. "What's up with you and Tony?" he asked.

Brandon turned toward his locker and began to dig through his bookbag and pull out some books. "Nothing," he mumbled.

"Char said that you told her you two got in a fight," Justin said. "But that's not what Tony told me."

Brandon turned back to Justin with fire in his eyes. "Makes sense," he said. "You *would* believe your good old buddy over me."

"Then tell me he's lying," Justin shot back.

For a second, Brandon looked like he was about to scream something at Justin. His eyes bulged, and he turned bright red. But instead, he looked down at his feet and toed the floor with one shoe.

"He's not," Brandon said.

"Then why tell Char that you two got in a fight?" Justin asked.

"Because they were being jerks to you," Brandon said. "I thought maybe . . . maybe you'd ditch them if I made up a story about how I got my black eye."

Justin knew he had a choice here. It was an important moment. He could make his friend feel bad about lying, or he could just let it go. That's kind of what he did with Tony when he found out the truth behind why he was being such a jerk. Justin felt Brandon deserved the same, so he made a joke out of it.

"Did you seriously smack yourself with your own gear?" Justin asked with a smile.

"Yeah," Brandon said, trying not to laugh. "Tony even tried to help me up off the ground. But I was too embarrassed."

"So you want in?" Justin asked, getting back to his original question.

Brandon's face went serious. He looked around the hallway. "Tony's not ticked off at me, is he?" he asked.

Justin shook his head no.

Brandon grinned. "Then I'm in," he said.

CHAPTER 10

HOME GAME

That week, for the first time since entering junior high, Justin felt like things were clicking for him. He had convinced his old friends to let his new friends join their band, The End Zonez.

Well, the name was still up for debate. Their band had changed from a power trio to quintet. They also needed to shift their music choice a little, to allow for a keyboardist and sax player. But all that seemed trivial.

Then Friday came. He showed up to school in a shirt and tie, and this time no one was shocked.

His band friends nodded as he walked past, and the football players high-fived him in the hallway.

It was a home game, so they didn't get out of their last period class. But Justin headed to the locker rooms right after.

Like before, he was on the field during the opening kickoff. He watched as their team's kicker stepped up to the ball and *poof!* It sailed through the air toward the other side of the field. Justin charged downfield. He heard the smacking of pads as bodies slammed together. Justin ran toward the kick returner but got pushed aside. Then the whistle blew, and the play was over.

On defense, Miles made a big play, tackling a runner just short of the first down, to stop the other team's drive. Then Justin was jogging onto the field for the punt return team. He heard someone shout, "Get 'em, JT."

Justin turned as Tony slapped him on the shoulder pads.

The Eagles got the ball after the punt. Coach Matthews went to work. It was run after run after run, slow and steady, grind-it-out football.

But as they neared their opponent's end zone, Coach Johnson called Justin's name. "Thomas!" he growled. "You're in."

Justin jogged on to the field and joined the offense's huddle.

The first play was a run. At the snap of the ball, Justin burst from his stance and slammed into the defender in front of him. He got his feet pumping to drive back the defender. The Eagles picked up only a couple yards on the play. Then they tried another run.

Justin could tell the other team was expecting it. Defenders were creeping up to the line, and when the ball was snapped, they overwhelmed the offensive line.

The Eagles were held for no gain.

In the huddle, Jorgenson looked over to the sideline as Coach Matthews signaled in the play.

"Eighty-four screen on two," Jorgenson said.

Justin smiled.

The huddle broke, and Justin strutted over to his position and got down in his stance. Across from him, he saw the defenders edging up to the line. They were expecting another run. But the call was a screen pass, and Justin was the target.

"Hut!" Jorgenson shouted.

Justin stayed perfectly still on the outside. On the inside, he was ready to explode, ready to take off downfield.

"Hut!" Jorgenson yelled.

The center hiked the ball to Jorgenson. He peddled backwards.

Justin exploded from his stance. He met the defensive end, knocked him to the side, and then stepped through the line of rushers.

Jorgenson scrambled to the left. So Justin drifted that way to make himself an easier target. Jorgenson lofted a pass over the upraised hands of several defenders. Justin was all alone when the ball reached him. He snagged it out of the air and brought it down, tucking it under one arm.

Justin rushed downfield. The end zone was just yards away. All that stood in his path was a defensive back.

Justin lowered his shoulder and charged, knocking the defender over and staying on his feet.

Touchdown!

ABOUT THE AUTHOR

Sports were always a part of Blake's life, whether he was bombing down a hill on his yellow penny board or cheering on his favorite football team (the Green Bay Packers). Today, he lives in St. Paul, Minnesota. He still rides a skateboard to get around and plays various sports from tennis to volleyball. When he's not playing or walking his dogs, he's writing. Blake has written more than one hundred books for young readers.

GLOSSARY

defense—the group of players who try to stop the opposing team from scoring

defensive back—a player on defense whose main job is to try to stop opposing players from catching passes and running down the field

defensive lineman—a player on defense whose main job is to try to stop the quarterback and tackle the running back; defensive linemen crouch down in front of the ball.

interception—when a defender catches a pass thrown by the opposing team

linebacker—a player on defense whose main job is to make tackles and stop catches; a linebacker stands just behind the defensive linemen.

offense—the group of players who try to move down the field and score

offensive lineman—a player on offense whose main jobs is to protect the quarterback and to block for running backs

playoffs—the games played after the regular season is over; playoff games determine the champion.

quarterback—a player on offense whose main job is to throw and hand off the ball

rivals—teams that have played many hard-fought games against each other

running back—an offensive player whose main job is to take handoffs from the quarterback and run with the football

tight end—an offense player whose main jobs are to catch passes from the quarterback and to block defensive players

wide receiver—a player on offense whose main job is to catch passes from the quarterback

DISCUSSION QUESTIONS

1. Throughout the story, Justin struggles with the choice between playing football with his old friends or playing in band with his new friends. Have you ever had to make a difficult choice between friends? Why did you have to make the choice, and what did you decide to do?

2. Brandon doesn't tell the truth about the incident between him and Tony. Instead, he lets people believe that Tony picked a fight and hit him. Why do you think he does this?

3. Imagine you were in a band. Would you choose to play with Tony and Miles or Char and Brandon? Why, and what type of the songs would you play?

WRITING PROMPTS

1. Imagine you were playing football with Justin, Tony, and Miles. Which position would you play? Write a story about a big game against your crosstown rivals. Who scores? Who makes some big plays? And who wins?

2. Imagine that you were a member of The End Zonez and needed a new song for an upcoming show. Write down the lyrics.

3. In seventh grade, Justin played in band, and in eighth grade he tried out for football. What do you think he will do in ninth grade? Write down your answer, and then describe your reasons for thinking that Justin would join band, play football, or do something else.

Tight ends are a hybrid of offense linemen and wide receivers. They have both blocking and pass catching responsibilities.

Originally, football did not have a tight end position. Players played both on defensive and offense. Receivers played as defensive backs, while blockers played as defensive lineman. But in the1940s and 1950s, players started specializing in either defensive or offense. Some players were good pass catchers but too big to be speedy receivers, and some were good blockers, but too small to be offensive linemen. So the position of tight end evolved to use their talents.

At first, most teams used tight ends more as an additional blocker. But in the 1960s, receiving tight ends like Mike Ditka and John Mackey shined. Today, big-play tight ends like Rob Gronkowski and Travis Kelce are threats to score on any given play.

PRO FOOTBALL TIGHT ENDS RECORDS

Most TDs in a Career: Tony Gonzalez and Antonio Gates (111)

Most TDs in a Season: Rob Gronkowski (17)

Most TDs in a Game: Kellen Winslow (5)

Most Receiving Yards in a Career: Tony Gonzalez (15,126)

Most Receiving Yards in a Season: Rob Gronkowski (1,327)

Most Receiving Yards in a Game: Shannon Sharpe (214)

Most Receptions in a Career: Tony Gonzalez (1,325)

Most Receptions in a Season: Tony Gonzalez (102)

Most Receptions in a Game: Jason Witten (18)